ABBY BYNE

CHERRY CHOCOLATE MURDER

A Tempting Mystery Unfolds
(2024 Desert Cookbook)

Copyright © 2024 by Abby Byne

All rights reserved. No part of this publication may be reproduced, stored or transmitted in any form or by any means, electronic, mechanical, photocopying, recording, scanning, or otherwise without written permission from the publisher. It is illegal to copy this book, post it to a website, or distribute it by any other means without permission.

First edition

This book was professionally typeset on Reedsy. Find out more at reedsy.com

Contents

Chapter 1	1
Chapter 2	4
Chapter 3	8
Chapter 4	11
Chapter 5	14
Chapter 6	16
Chapter 7	18
Chapter 8	21
Chapter 9	24
Chapter 10	27

Chapter 1

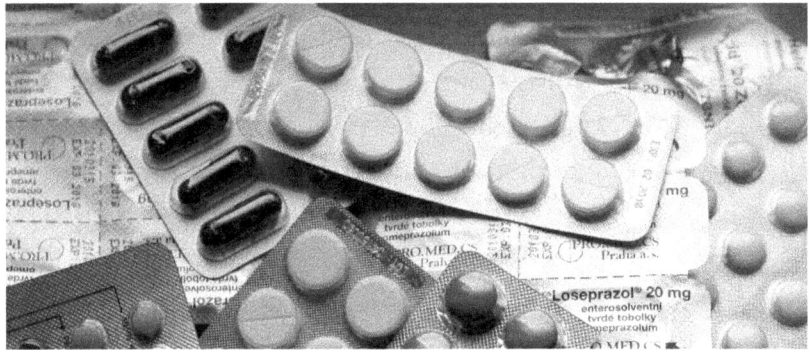

Bitsie's sister-in-law leaned in, curiosity evident in her eyes. "So, spill the beans! How was your evening with Nick?"

"Shh!" Bitsie hushed her, scanning the empty bakery kitchen cautiously. She and Liz were alone for now, but Nick could stroll in from the front counter at any moment. "It wasn't what you think," she whispered.

Liz feigned innocence. "What? Did I say something wrong?"

"It wasn't a date," Bitsie clarified firmly.

"But didn't you two go out for dinner and catch a movie?" Liz persisted, lowering her voice as Bitsie requested.

"We did," Bitsie admitted, "but it wasn't a date."

"Dinner and a movie sounds like a date to me," Liz insisted.

"It wasn't," Bitsie reiterated. "Nick and I are just friends."

"So, you've friend-zoned him?" Liz quipped.

Bitsie shook her head. "No, that's not it at all. If anyone's doing the friend-zoning, it's Nick. He's way too young for me, and besides, he's out of my league."

Liz raised an eyebrow, returning to her cupcake preparations. "Interesting. So, what's the deal with Anabel calling in sick so often lately?"

Bitsie frowned, contemplating. "It's not normal. She hardly ever called in sick when I first took over the bakery. Three times in three months seems off."

"Maybe she caught a bug she can't shake," Liz suggested.

Bitsie suspected otherwise, thinking James might be the real bug in Anabel's life, but she kept her thoughts to herself.

Nick poked his head into the kitchen, flashing a smile at Bitsie. She attempted a friendly response, affirming their friendship. "I'm closing up soon," Nick mentioned. "Will those cherry chocolate cupcakes be ready to box?"

"Off to see your granddad?" Liz inquired.

Nick nodded. "Every Tuesday. And I can't show up empty-handed. Cherry chocolate is his latest craving."

"I thought he didn't like chocolate," Bitsie interjected.

"He doesn't, but his new lady friend does," Nick explained.

Bitsie chuckled at the romantic escapades of senior citizens. "Assisted living isn't dampening Granddad's spirits, it seems."

Nick nodded, sharing tales of his grandfather's romantic entanglements. "He's managed to fall in love three times while I'm still trying to get over one."

Bitsie wanted to pry about Nick's past relationship, but she refrained. "Sounds like a love triangle," she remarked.

CHAPTER 1

Nick agreed, mentioning another suitor vying for Granddad's crush. "It's complicated," he sighed.

"Is Granddad wooing her with cupcakes?" Liz joked.

Nick confirmed it, adding, "But they haven't won her over yet."

They planned to visit Granddad, with Nick inviting Bitsie to grab a bite afterward. As they left for Shady Grove, Bitsie's mind wandered, contemplating the complexities of love.

At Shady Grove, they found Granddad amidst a card game, and introductions were made to Malcolm, a familiar but elusive figure. Despite the jovial atmosphere, Bitsie sensed tension in the air.

Afterward, Nick's demeanor shifted when he received a distressing call about Malcolm's health. Bitsie couldn't fathom Nick's reaction until she learned Malcolm had collapsed after consuming a cupcake they'd brought.

Concerned and bewildered, Bitsie realized there was more to this simple evening than meets the eye.

Chapter 2

"Roscoe mentioned they sent the cupcake for analysis," Roscoe said, his complexion drained, appearing shaken, and noticeably aged.

"By 'they,' do you mean the police?" Bitsie inquired. She contemplated whether to contact her brother Stan. Though retired from the local police force for seven months, he retained reserve status and might have pertinent information. However, she scolded herself, it wasn't her place to involve herself in potential crimes, nor was it Stan's. Besides, the situation didn't definitively suggest a crime had occurred. Bitsie also considered her sister-in-law, Liz, who had adamantly opposed Stan's continued involvement in solving mysteries following an incident involving an electrician's death in Bitsie's bakery kitchen. Liz reminded her that their retirement was meant to be shared. Understanding Liz's perspective, Bitsie refrained from involving Stan.

"The police visited earlier today," Roscoe continued. "Questioned everyone extensively and searched some of our rooms. I offered mine for search voluntarily, as I have nothing to hide."

"Did they discover anything?" Nick inquired.

"I'm unsure. They only took my trash. I can't fathom why they'd want that," Roscoe replied.

"What sort of questions did they pose?" Bitsie couldn't resist asking.

"They inquired about Malcolm's potential adversaries and recent disagreements," Roscoe responded. "He's had numerous conflicts, making it challenging to discern whose bad side he's earned."

"Have you and Malcolm argued recently?" Nick queried.

"Certainly. We've had our disagreements, especially over Lavinia," Roscoe admitted. "I warned him to back off, but it wasn't a serious threat. Just heat of the moment talk."

"Let's hope Malcolm didn't interpret it differently," Nick cautioned. "Accusations could arise, especially if the cupcake was poisoned."

"I understand," Roscoe sighed. "But I meant no harm."

"Who else has Malcolm argued with lately?" Bitsie inquired.

"Practically everyone, including a male CNA named James Johnson," Roscoe revealed. "Malcolm filed a complaint against him, alleging threats, but it's uncertain if they're valid."

"Why did Malcolm argue with James?" Bitsie pressed.

"James is abrasive, but Malcolm accused him of threats, including smothering him with a pillow," Roscoe disclosed. "However, it's uncertain if it truly occurred."

"Did anyone witness the alleged threat?" Bitsie probed.

"Malcolm claims Clarence Crake overheard it, but Clarence denies it," Roscoe explained.

"What's Clarence like?" Nick questioned.

"He's reserved but has been friendlier lately," Roscoe described. "He enjoys brief morning chats with me but keeps to himself otherwise."

"Is there anyone else who might have a grudge against Malcolm?" Nick inquired.

"Perhaps Ruby Sheers, who has shown a romantic interest in Malcolm," Roscoe suggested. "However, her behavior has been erratic lately, possibly due to mental decline."

"Why would Ruby want to harm Malcolm?" Bitsie wondered.

"Following a confrontation with Malcolm, she issued a menacing threat," Roscoe revealed. "It's uncertain if she's capable, but her recent behavior raises concerns."

As they left the hospital, Bitsie pondered, "What are your thoughts on the situation, Nick?"

"I doubt Granddad's involvement," Nick asserted. "But until we have more information…"

"We can't assume Malcolm was poisoned," Bitsie reasoned. "By the way, did you discover why Roscoe visited the clinic?"

"He had heart issues, possibly due to medication irregularity," Nick disclosed.

"Do you think he's becoming forgetful?" Bitsie questioned.

"Not likely. Roscoe's reliable," Nick assured.

"Strange," Bitsie mused.

"Agreed," Nick concurred.

"Should we visit Malcolm?" Bitsie proposed.

"It couldn't hurt," Nick agreed.

Two days later, they visited Malcolm at Shady Grove, finding him disgruntled. Despite his resentment, they offered him

CHAPTER 2

crossword puzzle books, attempting to brighten his spirits. However, Malcolm remained cynical, accusing Nick of attempting to harm him. Bitsie and Nick listened, grappling with Malcolm's accusations and the uncertainty surrounding the cupcake incident.

Chapter 3

"Are you back to your detective games?" Stan, Bitsie's brother, inquired with a hint of concern. "Are you sure it's wise to dive into this one, especially considering your connection with Nick—"

Stan's sentence trailed off, and Bitsie suspected Liz had given him a discreet nudge under the table.

"Delicious pasta!" Liz interjected, swiftly changing the subject. "What's the secret herb in the pesto? Tarragon?"

"Yeah, I have a big tarragon plant out front. I dried some last summer," Bitsie replied.

Bitsie adored her garden. Despite her tiny cottage, the backyard compensated for it. Even in November, the mild weather made it an ideal spot for an alfresco Sunday lunch. The patio stones reflected the midday sun, creating a warm ambiance.

CHAPTER 3

Max, their pet, lounged just inside the French doors, basking in the sunlight and observing the humans indulge in pasta.

Stan persisted, returning to the topic of the poisoned cupcake. "Don't divulge anything! It's troublesome enough that you're involved," Liz cautioned Bitsie.

"I'm not deeply involved," Bitsie defended. "I haven't even mentioned Malcolm's suspicions about Roscoe's medication."

Stan intervened, teasingly remarking, "Where there's a murder, there's Bitsie."

"But there hasn't been a murder," Bitsie clarified. "And Liz, don't worry, I won't drag Stan into this."

However, Stan revealed, "Actually, I might already be involved. Jones had to step back from the case due to his wife's delivery, so they've asked me to pitch in during his paternity leave."

"Humph!" Liz huffed in response.

"Surely, you don't oppose people having babies?" Stan teased Liz. "I thought you were always pro-baby."

Turning back to the investigation, Bitsie inquired, "So, an official investigation is underway?"

"The lab results won't be back for another two weeks," Stan informed them. "Feel free to poke around Shady Grove in the meantime."

As they discussed the case further, Anabel returned to work the next day, behaving oddly. Bitsie noticed her change in attire and attempted to glean information from her about James and the cupcake incident.

However, they were interrupted by a customer, leaving Bitsie unable to question Anabel further. Later, Bitsie and Nick discussed Roscoe's involvement in the case, causing concern for both of them.

Despite Nick's worries, Bitsie tried to reassure him. "Even if the cupcake contained Roscoe's medication, it doesn't necessarily implicate him."

Their conversation delved into the intricacies of the case, but Bitsie resolved to visit Shady Grove to gather more information.

Chapter 4

Upon her arrival at Shady Grove, Bitsie didn't immediately set off to find Roscoe. They had arranged to meet in the common room at six, but Bitsie had intentionally arrived earlier, hoping to catch Ruby Sheers in a talkative mood. Spotting Ruby by the windows, where Roscoe had mentioned Miss Lavinia Fay often frequented, Bitsie wondered if Miss Fay would appear and what the two women might discuss.

Initially, Ruby didn't recognize Bitsie. After a tedious explanation, Ruby finally recalled, "Oh yes, you're Nick's girlfriend." Tempted to deny it, Bitsie refrained, having just clarified her connection to Roscoe's grandson. This served as an opening for Bitsie to inquire about Ruby's romantic life.

As Bitsie probed, Ruby's demeanor shifted abruptly from agreeable to frightening, followed by a barrage of obscenities. Despite her initial appearance as a sweet old lady, Ruby evidently had a darker side, directed particularly at a man who had spurned her, presumably Malcolm.

Suspicious of Bitsie's intentions, Ruby accused her of spying, fueled by paranoia over Malcolm's involvement. Bitsie denied the accusation, while internally acknowledging her covert observation.

Later, in a moment of candor, Ruby implicated Miss Lavinia Fay as the culprit behind Malcolm's troubles, citing a past relationship with another man during August. This revelation surprised Bitsie, as no one had previously suggested Miss Fay's involvement.

Curiosity piqued, Bitsie probed further, contemplating Ruby's credibility and Miss Fay's motives. Their conversation shifted to Roscoe, with Bitsie learning about his unrequited affection for Miss Fay.

Exiting the common room with Roscoe, Bitsie sensed curious eyes on them. They discussed Miss Fay's past as an opera singer before Bitsie diverted the conversation to Roscoe's heart medication.

Later, at the bakery, Bitsie overheard a tense exchange between Nick and a woman named Tracy, presumably his ex-wife. Feeling a pang of jealousy, Bitsie left, determined to unravel the mystery surrounding Malcolm's poisoning.

Researching Roscoe's medication, Bitsie discovered its potential link to Malcolm's condition, realizing the ease with which

CHAPTER 4

a dosage mix-up could occur. This revelation propelled her closer to uncovering the truth behind Malcolm's collapse.

Chapter 5

The following morning, Bitsie finally encountered Anabel's elusive boyfriend, James. Arriving at ten, Bitsie noticed Anabel's car missing from its usual spot. Hoping Anabel hadn't skipped work without notice, Bitsie found her hard at work frosting cupcakes from that morning's bake.

"You didn't bring your car today?" Bitsie inquired.

"It wouldn't start," Anabel replied. "Hector gave me a ride, and James will pick me up soon."

Concerned, Anabel hinted at leaving early due to uncertainty about James's arrival time and his impatience. Bitsie reassured her before retreating to the office.

Bitsie sensed Anabel's unease; it was unusual for her to leave work early, but she seemed more fearful of James's reaction than any work consequences. Soon, she heard Anabel arguing

CHAPTER 5

with a man in the alley.

"Why call him instead of me? Are you seeing him?" the man accused.

Anabel explained Hector's convenience, but the man's sarcasm escalated into abusive language. Unable to stand by, Bitsie intervened, only to witness James grabbing Anabel by the throat.

Summoning help, Bitsie dialed 911, prompting James to flee after threatening retaliation. Despite Anabel's reluctance, Bitsie insisted on involving the authorities, knowing it was the right thing.

Later, over dinner with Stan and Liz, they discussed the frustration of powerless intervention in such cases. Stan predicted further trouble from James.

Indeed, days later, James's violent tendencies resurfaced at the care facility where he attacked Malcolm, prompting police intervention. Bitsie suspected James's involvement in previous incidents, including Malcolm's poisoning.

Offering Anabel refuge, Bitsie urged her to seek legal protection. Anabel denied James's involvement in the poisoning, citing their alibi. Although skeptical, Bitsie acknowledged the complexity of the situation.

Anabel's phone revealed a timeline corroborating her alibi. Despite doubts, Bitsie couldn't dismiss Anabel's defense entirely. Their conversation turned to a witness, Cherise, who could provide additional insights into James's actions.

Overall, Bitsie remained wary of James's potential danger and determined to support Anabel through the ordeal.

Chapter 6

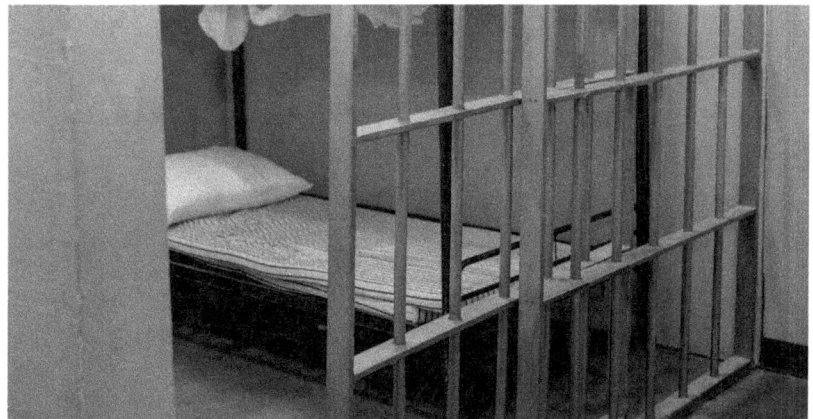

James was detained for only a day before being released on bail, but during that time, Anabel disappeared. Her sister in Chicago had invited her for a two-week stay, and Anabel took up the offer, encouraged by Bitsie. Bitsie assured her that her job would still be waiting upon her return. Just before leaving for Chicago, Anabel took legal steps to file for a restraining order against James.

Despite Anabel's departure, Bitsie couldn't shake off her unease. She remained suspicious of James's involvement in Malcolm's poisoning. Exhausted from covering Anabel's shift at the bakery, Bitsie headed to Shady Grove to find Cherise. She

CHAPTER 6

hoped Cherise could corroborate Anabel's claim that James was away from the scene during the critical time. At Shady Grove, she visited Roscoe, who lamented Nick's absence.

Nick had been distant lately, especially since the arrival of a woman from Nebraska. Their interactions had dwindled, and Nick avoided discussing the poisoning case. Meanwhile, the police investigation hadn't progressed much, with Stan keeping tight-lipped about it.

Bitsie learned Cherise was off that day but might be attending her brother's birthday party at Brink's Lake. Though hesitant about another visit there, Bitsie decided to go. Before leaving Shady Grove, she checked on Malcolm, who showed her a threatening note he'd received, hinting at trouble with Miss Fay.

At Brink's Lake, Bitsie located the birthday party and eventually approached Cherise. After some initial wariness, Cherise recognized Bitsie and engaged in conversation. Bitsie cautiously probed about James's whereabouts during the cupcake incident, hoping Cherise could provide alibi confirmation.

Cherise remained tight-lipped due to patient confidentiality but hinted at security camera footage as evidence. Despite Stan's reticence, Bitsie shared her findings with him over dinner. Stan, intrigued but skeptical, urged her to reveal more.

Later, Liz's revelation about Nick potentially rekindling with his ex-wife left Bitsie disheartened. She struggled with conflicting emotions but ultimately decided to focus on moving forward. Sharing ice cream with her cat Max, she resolved to face the situation head-on and indulge in some chocolate sauce for comfort.

Chapter 7

Stan's voice came through the phone, affirming, "You were correct." Bitsie nearly fumbled the pastry bag filled with banana cream as she heard Stan's admission. She didn't need to inquire about what she was right about. "Anything else I should be aware of?" she probed.

"Nope," Stan replied before abruptly ending the call, leaving no room for further questioning.

With James having an alibi, Bitsie's suspect list narrowed

considerably. While she didn't rule out Ruby entirely, the evidence against her was scant regarding the poisoned cupcake. However, one individual piqued Bitsie's curiosity — Miss Lavinia Fay, the central figure in the ordeal. It was high time Bitsie confronted Miss Fay to extract some answers.

Contemplating whether Nick still delivered treats to his grandfather, Bitsie decided it was time to revive that tradition. After finishing the banana cream cupcakes, she boxed them up, anticipating Nick's arrival. Though it was early for her to leave, she resolved to avoid Nick for the time being, sensing a reluctance within herself.

Carrying the box of cupcakes, Bitsie discreetly exited through the back door, notifying Hector, who was restocking the shelves, of her early departure. Concerns lingered about the bakery's declining business post-poisoning, despite no direct accusations. Until the truth about the cupcake incident emerged, potential customers remained wary.

Bitsie's frequent visits to Shady Grove had made her familiar with the receptionists. Sue, one of the receptionists, casually inquired about her destination. Although Bitsie wasn't headed to see Roscoe, she nodded along to avoid appearing overly inquisitive.

"Malcolm's been asking for you," Sue added. This revelation surprised Bitsie, given her strained relationship with Malcolm.

Upon reaching Miss Fay's room, Bitsie engaged in conversation, with Miss Fay mistaking her for Nick's girlfriend. Bitsie corrected the misunderstanding, opting for a vague response about her relationship with Nick. As they conversed, Bitsie noticed a teddy bear in the room, which Lavinia revealed was a gift for her grandson.

The conversation shifted to Malcolm's poisoning, with

Lavinia disclosing receiving anonymous love letters since September. Bitsie proposed catching the sender in the act, but logistical constraints made it difficult. However, examining the letters, Bitsie noticed similarities to a threatening letter she had borrowed from Malcolm. Recognizing a potential lead, she requested to take the letters home for further analysis.

Chapter 8

Before departing Shady Grove with Lavinia's bundle of eerie love letters, Bitsie made a detour to Roscoe's room. While Lavinia hadn't explicitly instructed Bitsie to keep mum about the love letters, she assumed it was implied. Moreover, Bitsie had no intention of spreading gossip about the threatening note Malcolm had received. She surmised that the author of these letters must be a resident at Shady Grove. Catching them in the act would be easier if they remained unaware of anyone trying to expose them.

Bitsie pondered why Lavinia hadn't taken her concerns to the staff. Shouldn't they be responsible for safeguarding residents from harassment? Additionally, Malcolm's reluctance to involve the police puzzled her. Perhaps, Bitsie mused, elderly folks stuck together, refraining from snitching on each other despite internal conflicts.

Though intriguing, this theory didn't explain why Lavinia and Malcolm had confided in her instead of seeking out someone with proper authority. Finding Roscoe absent from his room, Bitsie discovered him in the common area with Clarence Crake, both engrossed in their own activities. Attempting to engage Clarence in conversation, Bitsie proposed a game of chess, hoping to uncover more about him. However, Clarence declined, expressing a desire to be left alone, prompting Roscoe to suggest a game of checkers instead.

A tense exchange ensued when Roscoe attempted to retrieve the chess set, revealing an unexpected confrontation between Roscoe and Clarence over its ownership. Despite Bitsie's attempts to defuse the situation, neither man relented, leaving her puzzled by Clarence's fear and possessiveness regarding the chess set.

Afterward, Bitsie sought answers from Clarence but found his room locked. Faintly hearing a repetitive recording from within, reminiscent of a message she had heard before, Bitsie left, deciding to investigate Malcolm's situation instead.

CHAPTER 8

Retrieving the threat-letter from her bag, she confirmed its delivery and texted Nick about it before leaving Shady Grove.

The following day, Bitsie forced herself to remain at the bakery, feeling exhausted from her late-night investigation of the love letters. When Nick exhibited unusual behavior upon her return, Bitsie's suspicions grew, prompting her to undertake clandestine activities at Shady Grove, including dumpster diving for potential evidence related to recent events.

Chapter 9

That night, after serving Max his dinner, Bitsie secured him in the bedroom and laid out a fresh sheet in the living room. Placing the retrieved trash bag from the dumpster at the center, she gloved up and meticulously emptied its contents onto the sheet, inspecting each item. Within twenty minutes, she was certain she had found the culprit. Just as she prepared to call Stan, her phone rang—it was Nick.

"I just got a call from a lawyer representing Granddad," Nick informed her. "He was arrested at Shady Grove this afternoon."

"But he's innocent," Bitsie insisted.

"I want to believe that too, but lab results suggest otherwise. The substance in the poisoned cupcake matches Granddad's heart medication."

"But others at Shady Grove take the same medication," Bitsie pointed out.

"That's true, but there's more," Nick continued. "After the incident, Granddad allowed a search of his room, where they found another tampered cupcake in his trashcan."

"Maybe it was accidental," Bitsie suggested.

"It's unlikely. The cupcake in his trashcan was clearly tampered with, containing traces of the same medication."

"Could Granddad have done it?"

"I don't want to think so, but without witnesses to prove he never left the common room, it doesn't look good."

"What's Granddad's story?"

"He claims he never left the common room that evening except to use the bathroom."

"Proving that might be challenging," Bitsie acknowledged.

"I know," Nick sighed.

"So, your theory is someone framed Granddad?"

"Yes, unless he's genuinely guilty. I hate to doubt him, but finding another tainted cupcake in his trash is damning."

"I'm convinced he's innocent," Bitsie asserted. "And I have evidence."

"Really?" Nick sounded surprised.

"Yes, and I'm about to turn it over to the police."

Half an hour later, Stan examined the trash-laden floor in Bitsie's living room, puzzled. "What am I looking at here?"

Bitsie explained the contents and pointed out the significance of each item, including the odd brown goo and hollowed chess pieces.

"Interesting," Stan remarked, intrigued by her discoveries.

Bitsie then revealed her suspicion of Clarence Crake as the real culprit and his possible connection with Lavinia Fay. Stan agreed to investigate further, planning to search Clarence's room the next morning.

Later, as Bitsie pondered over the case, she realized Clarence's likely motive and modus operandi. She shared her insights with Nick, who was surprised by her deductions.

The next morning, armed with evidence, they prepared to confront Clarence. But before they could proceed, Bitsie sought a private moment with Nick, where emotions came to a head, and their relationship took an unexpected turn.

In the midst of the turmoil, Bitsie remained determined to see justice served, but uncertainties lingered as they braced for the confrontation ahead.

Chapter 10

Upon searching Clarence Crake's room, Bitsie found exactly what she had hoped for. The torn teddy bear retrieved from the dumpster revealed crucial evidence. Coupled with a stack of letters indicating motive and intent, Clarence confessed to attempting to murder Malcolm Smith. Although released on bail, Shady Grove declined to take him back pending trial, so Clarence was sent to live with his niece and elderly sister in Little Rock until his court date. Bitsie could only hope they secured their medicine cabinet.

Anabel returned to work after spending two weeks with her sister. While James awaited trial, Anabel obtained a restraining order and moved in with her cousin and her cousin's husband, a former Navy SEAL. This arrangement eased Bitsie's worries about her safety.

Stan assured Bitsie that both Clarence and James would likely be convicted, with Clarence possibly pleading insanity due to his declining mental state. Stan predicted Clarence would end up in a secure facility resembling Shady Grove rather than a conventional prison.

As Thanksgiving neared, Bitsie debated whether to visit her daughter in Dallas or celebrate with Stan and Liz in Little Creek. However, both plans fell through unexpectedly. Stan and Liz opted for a last-minute Caribbean cruise without inviting Bitsie, and Emily postponed dinner due to illness.

Disappointed and feeling lonely, Bitsie contemplated spending Thanksgiving alone. She imagined absurd scenarios like crafting a turkey out of cat food. Thoughts of Nick, who had expressed his feelings for her, crossed her mind. Despite uncertainty about starting a new relationship, she decided to reach out to Nick for a date.

Nick, initially surprised by her invitation, suggested they spend Thanksgiving together since his family plans were minimal. Bitsie hesitated, feeling their situation wasn't typical for a first date. However, Nick reassured her, acknowledging their unconventional status.

Feeling flustered, Bitsie ended the call, realizing her forwardness may have been presumptuous. She joked about being the biggest turkey before planning Thanksgiving dinner at her place. Despite her embarrassment, she looked forward to preparing a traditional meal and decorating for the holidays, although she reconsidered the idea of a Christmas tree due to limited space.

www.ingramcontent.com/pod-product-compliance
Lightning Source LLC
LaVergne TN
LVHW020453080526
838202LV00055B/5435